SUSAN TEWS

NETTIE'S GIFT

Illustrated by

ELIZABETH SAYLES

CLARION BOOKS

New York

Clarion Books
a Houghton Mifflin Company imprint
215 Park Avenue South, New York, NY 10003
Text copyright © 1993 by Susan Tews
Illustrations copyright © 1993 by Elizabeth Sayles

Printed in the U.S.A.

Library of Congress Cataloging-in-Publication Data

Tews, Susan.
Nettie's gift / by Susan Tews : illustrated by Elizabeth Sayles.
p.   cm.
Summary: On a visit to Grandma Nettie's, a little girl acquires an
imaginary playmate who is very much like her grandmother as a child.
ISBN 0-395-59027-2
[1. Grandmothers—Fiction.   2. Imaginary playmates—Fiction.]
I. Sayles, Elizabeth, ill.   II. Title.
PZ7.T29647Ne   1993
[E]—dc20   91-32988
                                                          CIP
                                                          AC

WOZ   10   9   8   7   6   5   4   3   2   1

For my grandmother,
Bernice Sopata
— *S. T.* —

To Ellen and Anne,
and to Alexandra
— *E. S.* —

It's a billowy autumn afternoon
when I decide to walk to Grandma Nettie's.
The air smells crackly,
so I know it's a good day
for hickory nut hunting.
My mother hangs up the phone.
She says, "Wear your winter coat, Sarah.
It's nippy out."
My ears tickle
inside the fuzzy hood.
I stuff a bread bag in my pocket
and I'm on my way.

Where can Barney be?
When I whistle
he comes running.
I toss a stick for him
and yell, "Fetch, boy!"
Grandma and Grandpa's farm
is the next one over from ours,
but it's a long walk
past rows and rows of corn stubble.

Barney brings back the stick
and drops it at my feet.
He gives me a breathy dog grin.
If a friend lived nearby
we could take turns
throwing the stick to Barney.
We could jump rope and play tag,
and I would tell her stories.
But Barney's about my only friend
who doesn't live far away.
I ruffle his fur
and hug his warm neck.

Grandma is waiting for me outside.
She says, "Your mother asked me
to find you a good hickory tree."
Grandma and I walk together way out back.
She says, "There used to be a shaggy hickory
near the old house where I grew up,
what's left of it."
Barney runs off ahead of us.
The path is covered over now
with weeds and barbed wire.
The trees lean together,
almost hiding this place.

But when you get up close,
the branches open into two rows,
and it's like walking under a grand archway
beneath reds as bright as paint
with shimmery gold and orange swirled in.
Grandma takes my hands in hers
and rubs them until they feel warm.
I forgot my mittens, but I don't care about that.
I tell her, "I wish I had someone to play with."
She says, "When I was a little girl,
I played alone almost every day.
But first I had to do chores...."

Then Grandma gets a remembering look.
She says, "When I was eight, like you,
one of my jobs was to water
our two big workhorses."
The leaves swish over our feet.
I feel the old wagon-wheel ruts
through the soles of my shoes
as I listen to Grandma talk.
Soon she says, "There's your hickory tree."
She looks around for a minute,
then tells me, "See you back at the house."
I wave good-bye.
I think it's peaceful,
like being in a palace,
this secret place in the woods.

There's a speckled blue tin cup
lying next to the old water pump.
I try out the handle. It squeaks.
It leaves nutmeg-colored
rust on my hands.
The handle must have made
this same sound
when my grandma was a little girl
pumping water for the horses.
I can almost hear her father calling,
"Nettie! Nettie!
Finish your chores!"
I think I hear her giggling.
Maybe she'd rather play
than do her work.

I start to play hopscotch
on the bumpy concrete slab.
I pretend little Nettie is playing with me.
Her long braid flops in the air
each time she jumps.
I laugh loud enough for two.

There's a sound like the ocean
that makes me look up.
I tell Nettie
the dry hickory leaves above
want our attention.
We feel dizzy
but we can't help
looking higher.
The branches pose
like a hundred ballet dancers
with skinny fingers entwined.
Sunlight glistens off the leaves
like big sequins
on fluffy skirts.

Below, tree roots clench the earth.
We search for hickory nuts.
They look like tiny cream-colored pumpkins
against the dark ground.
But we only find a handful.
My bread bag is hardly full at all.

Then Nettie takes my hand
and pulls me back to the pump.
There is a surprise waiting—
a huge pile of hickory nuts!
Where did they come from?
Nettie grins.
Could she have gathered them
for me in the woods?
It takes me three tries with a rock
to crack open one shell,
but it's worth the work.
The bumpy nut inside
tastes better than wild strawberries,
better than snap peas from the vine,
better than falling snow on your tongue.
I break one open for Nettie.
I tell her, "Thank you so much
for the hickory nuts!"

The wind blows our hair.
The air is turning gray.
Ducks fly up
from deep in the woods.
They rise in a misty column
making throaty quacks.
I'm feeling a little alone again.
I'm glad when Barney
comes back huffing
from chasing rabbits.
Barney and I start walking.
I see Grandma and Grandpa's house.
The lights are on in the kitchen.
I smell roast beef cooking.
My cheeks are cold
and my toes are numb,
and I just want to get there.

But I can't run as fast as Barney.
He beats me to the house.
Grandpa is outside.
He gives Barney an ear-scratching.
When I get to Grandpa, he says,
"Well, well, if it isn't our little Sarah."
Then he calls to my grandma
in his gravelly voice,
"Nettie!"
It sounds like a distant
familiar echo.
"Nettie!"
I see Grandma Nettie
in the kitchen window
watching for me.
The light bounces
off the top of her glasses.

She smiles and she says,
"You were gone so long."
I say, "I found a friend!
She was make-believe
but we had a wonderful time.
And you know what else?
Look what she gave me!"
I show her the proof,
my bulging sack of hickory nuts.
Grandma says, "A make-believe friend?
Imagine that."
Grandma Nettie's eyes sparkle
in her mischievous way.
She says, "Why, your old grandma
still knows where to find
the best hickory trees."

Suddenly, I recognize
little Nettie's eyes in hers.
"Grandma," I say,
"*You* gave me the hickory nuts!"
She just smiles.
Barney scampers into the kitchen
as Grandpa closes the porch door softly.
I give Grandma Nettie my best bear hug.